THE EXTRAORDINARY FILES

Gene Machine

Paul Blum

RISING★STARS

'The truth is inside us.
It is the only place where it can hide.'

nasen

NASEN House, 4/5 Amber Business Village, Amber Close,
Amington, Tamworth, Staffordshire B77 4RP

Rising Stars UK Ltd.
22 Grafton Street, London W1S 4EX
www.risingstars-uk.com

Text © Rising Stars UK Ltd.
The right of Paul Blum to be identified as the author of this work has
been asserted by him in accordance with the Copyright, Design and
Patents Act 1988.

Published 2007

Cover design: Button plc
Illustrator: Enzo Troiano
Text design and typesetting: pentacorbig
Publisher: Gill Budgell
Editor: Maoliosa Kelly
Editorial consultants: Lorraine Petersen and Cliff Moon

British Library Cataloguing in Publication Data.
A CIP record for this book is available from the British Library.

ISBN: 978-1-84680-252-2

Printed by Craft Print International Limited, Singapore

CHAPTER ONE

A University Research Laboratory

Professor Hall was working late in his laboratory.
It was past midnight. As he packed his briefcase,
he heard something move in the corner of the lab.
He went over to see what it was.

A tall woman stepped from the shadows. Professor Hall turned very pale.

"What are you doing here, Jane?" he asked nervously.

"I've come to see my birthplace," she replied.

"There's nothing for you to see," he said. "You must go now or I'll have to call security."

"You'll be wasting your time," said Jane. "Take a look at the security screen."

The professor saw two guards lying dead on the floor by the entrance to the lab.

Professor Hall tried to run but the woman grabbed him by his tie.

"Oh no, you don't," she hissed. "I want a guided tour of my family home. I want you to show me the test tubes that are my real father and mother."

Then she picked him up and threw him across the room. He stood up slowly and came towards her shakily.

"What do you want to see?" he asked.

"Everything," she replied.

Parker and Turnbull were Secret Service Agents working for MI5. They had been called to the lab, where Professor Hall worked.

"What a terrible mess!" said Agent Turnbull. "There's broken glass everywhere and I wonder what that funny smell is?"

"It's cooling agent from these jars which contained embryo life forms," Agent Parker said.

"Whoever killed Professor Hall was very strong," Agent Turnbull pointed out. "His body looks like a broken doll."

"And they must have let all the animals out of the cages," said Agent Parker.

9

"We can see the murderer on the security screen," Parker said. "She's a very tall woman. Look at her. She must be three metres tall."

"Look at her neck," said Agent Turnbull. "It's as long as a giraffe!"

Suddenly, Parker looked serious.

"I think I know what's going on here, Laura," he said. "We need to speak to Commander Watson back in headquarters before we go any further with our investigation."

CHAPTER TWO

MI5 Headquarters, Vauxhall, London

Agents Turnbull and Parker went to see their boss, Commander Watson. He briefed them about Professor Hall's murderer.

"Professor Hall was murdered by Jane Wells. She's one of the leaders of a group of people who are against animal experiments. They've been attacking labs all over the country and killing the scientists who experiment on animals. They're a very dangerous group and they must be stopped."

"So what do we need to do next?" asked Turnbull.

"You must track down Jane and her two friends. We think they may try to attack scientists attending the Gene Genius Conference," Watson explained.

"The Gene Genius Conference is the biggest gathering of genetic scientists in the world," Parker said. "It's the place where all those who experiment with DNA come together and it's taking place this weekend in London."

"Yes, that's the one," Commander Watson said. "I want you to go to the Gene Genius Conference and pretend to be scientists. We'll get you the ID you need."

Back in his office, Parker put his feet on the desk and stared out of the window.

"So we're looking for Jane Wells and her two friends," he said.

"Who are her two friends?" Turnbull asked.

"Linda Lewis and David Munro," Parker explained. "The three of them work for an organisation called 'Animals Come First.'"

"Animals Come First," she repeated. "My cat would agree with that."

"The group believes that using animals for experiments is wrong, even if it may help cure terrible diseases like cancer and AIDS," he explained.

Turnbull read the file Watson had given her.

"The man that Jane Wells killed was a first-rate scientist," Turnbull said. "Professor Hall specialised in stem cell technology. It says in Watson's file that he made mutants. What's a mutant then, Agent Parker?"

"It's a creature made from mixing human genes and animal genes together. Its DNA is almost super-human. A mutant has the strength and power of an animal with the brain power of a human being. Most of the research into mutants is top secret. In fact, the government has banned research into mixing human genes with animal genes."

"I see," said Turnbull. "So Professor Hall's research was top secret. Can you imagine what a mutant would look like?"

"I think I can," he replied. He began to blow up the picture of Jane Wells on his computer. "Something like this …"

"A cross between a human and a giraffe!" she cried. "Perhaps Jane Wells and the people who want to stop the animal experiments are actually mutants themselves!"

Agent Parker nodded. "I think you may be right, Agent Turnbull. We're going to be looking for three very angry people …"

"… who may want to take revenge on the scientists who've ruined their lives," she said. "We get all the good jobs don't we, Parker?"

"We need to work fast, Laura, if we want to find out the truth," said Agent Parker. "The Secret Service may take us off this case. It's a big one. It may be a case for 'The Extraordinary Files'."

CHAPTER THREE

The Gene Genius Conference, London

Professor Lee had just finished her lecture. Everyone was clapping when a woman stepped forward, holding out a bunch of flowers.

"You are my mother. I have a present for you." said the woman.

There was a noise like a parrot squawking and the woman knocked Professor Lee to the ground and pecked her to death before running out of the room.

Parker and Turnbull arrived just as everyone was screaming.

"This looks like the work of a mutant," said Parker.

"Half human, half bird," Turnbull replied. "I think we're on the right track, Parker."

Turnbull and Parker looked at the security film of Professor Lee's murder again. Then they looked at the photograph of the three members of the organisation called Animals Come First.

"This time the murderer looks like Linda Lewis," said Parker.

"So that just leaves David Munro," said Turnbull. "We must find him before another murder takes place."

"Let's go to the last day of the Gene Genius Conference," Parker said, "I've a funny feeling we'll meet David Munro there."

CHAPTER FOUR

MI5 Headquarters, Vauxhall, London

Meanwhile, in a darkened room at MI5 headquarters, some very important people were meeting. There were four people in the room. One of them was Commander Watson, who looked nervous and uncomfortable. Sitting in the shadows, was a man. Everybody watched his hands as he polished his glasses until they shone.

"What do Agents Parker and Turnbull know?" demanded the man, whose hands never stopped moving.

"They don't know anything important," said Commander Watson.

The man in the shadows wasn't happy with this answer. He polished his glasses again then he started to tap them on the table. It sounded like a drum beating.

"They don't know anything important!?" he sneered. "They shouldn't know anything at all! You've messed up, Watson!"

The people in the room said nothing. Commander Watson had his head down. The tapping on the table got louder and faster. Then the man's glasses broke.

"Look what you've made me do!" shouted the man. "You'll pay for this. I want Agents Parker and Turnbull stopped. They know too much. I want them eliminated!"

"But X, Parker and Turnbull are our own agents!" Commander Watson said.

He was the only person in the room brave enough to speak. The man in the shadows laughed.

"Stop being so weak, Watson. Use the mutants to do the job. They've been trained to kill, after all."

CHAPTER FIVE

The Gene Genius Conference, London

Agent Parker had gone to a lecture on DNA while Agent Turnbull waited for him in the café. As she drank her hot chocolate she saw Jane Wells talking to David Munro.

"She looks just like a giraffe and he looks just like a monkey," she thought to herself.

Suddenly, Jane Wells and David Munro walked quickly towards the lift.

"I must follow them. Parker will just have to find me when he gets out," Turnbull said to herself as she stood up. She watched as David Munro and Jane Wells took the lift up to the 120th floor.

"That must be the roof garden," she thought, looking at a map of the building. "I'll jump in the next lift and see what they're up to."

27

The roof garden
was beautiful. It had
fountains, a stream and
a sundial. Agent Turnbull
hid behind some yellow
sunflowers.

"There they are!"
she whispered to herself.

Jane Wells was stretching
up her long neck to
eat some of the flower
blossoms.

David Munro swung
along the branches of
the trees before jumping
down in front of Jane
and beating his chest with
his long hairy arms.

Then they saw Turnbull.

"Er, I was just taking a breath of fresh air," Turnbull said nervously.

"I was just having a light lunch," said Jane Wells, smiling. "There was nothing on the menu that I fancied."

"And I needed to get some exercise," David Munro added. "The seats in the lecture room make my back hurt."

As the two mutants moved closer to Turnbull, she felt a shiver of fear go down her spine. She walked quickly back to the lift. As she tried to shut the door, Jane Wells jammed her long neck into it.

"Wait for me, Agent Turnbull," she said.

The doors opened and Jane Wells and David Munro
jumped into the lift, snarling at her. Turnbull backed
away from both of them. She pulled out her gun
and held up her ID card.

"I'm a secret agent and you are both under arrest for murder!" she shouted.

They just laughed at her.

"That's what you think," said Jane. "But my friend Linda has other ideas."

Suddenly a large bird flew into the lift straight at Turnbull. She fell backwards and knocked her head on the floor. Everything went black and she passed out with the three mutants standing over her.

CHAPTER SIX

When Agent Turnbull came to, she was lying on Parker's sofa.

"What's going on? I can't remember anything," she said.

"I drove you here. You're safe now, Laura," Parker replied.

"You saved my life. I was sure that those three mutants were going to kill me," she said in a weak voice.

"Yes, I think they were," he said. "But I can't work out why they want to kill you. You aren't one of the scientists who brought them to life or who does experiments on animals."

"Perhaps it's because I saw them in their animal form in the roof garden?" she said.

"Perhaps," he said. "But I think there's something more sinister going on. I think they wanted to kill both of us and they wanted to keep it a secret. When I arrived in the other lift they began to attack me but they ran off when two window cleaners appeared."

"So we are still in danger," she said weakly. He nodded.

At that moment, there was a banging on the door of Parker's flat and the windows rattled. Parker's flat was on the third floor.

"Quickly," he said. "The mutants are back. Come with me. There's only one way out, down the rubbish slide in the kitchen," he explained.

"You must be joking, Parker," she said. "I'm not getting into that dirty hole. What will I look like when I come out the other end?"

"Not as bad as you'll look if the mutants get you," he replied. "Just go!"

They went down the slide and landed in the metal dustbins. Quickly, they climbed out and got into Agent Turnbull's car.

"Where are we going?" she asked.

"We've got to get to HQ and tell them what's been going on. I think our lives are in danger," replied Agent Parker.

CHAPTER SEVEN

MI5 Headquarters, Vauxhall, London

Commander Watson listened to their story.

"You did the right thing to come and see me. I can tell you that just before you got here, a team of special agents shot the three mutants dead. They surrounded them in Agent Parker's garden. It was a clever idea to escape in the rubbish slide but I could have saved you a dry cleaning bill. We were just about to rescue you."

Agent Turnbull smiled. She was glad that the mutants had been shot. Agent Parker didn't smile. He didn't believe Commander Watson's story.

"When can we see the three bodies?" he asked.

Commander Watson looked nervous. "That's not possible, Agent Parker. The case has been taken out of our hands. The bodies were taken away. It's a top-secret investigation now."

"I understand," said Parker. But it was easy to see that he didn't understand at all.

Nothing made sense to him anymore. He didn't trust Commander Watson and he knew that he and Turnbull were still in danger.

When Agents Turnbull and Parker had left the room, Commander Watson turned to a man sitting in the shadows.

"Did I say the right thing?" he asked. "Do you think they know too much?"

The man in the shadows was polishing his glasses. It was too dark to see his eyes.

"Watson, you're learning fast. Let's leave them alone – for now."

"And the three mutants, Wells, Lewis and Munro?" asked Commander Watson. "Are they really … ?"

He was too afraid to finish his sentence. The man in the shadows polished his glasses so hard that it sounded like a drum banging on the table.

The conversation was definitely over.

GLOSSARY OF TERMS

cooling agent fluid which keeps things cool

DNA deoxyribonucleic acid, the code of life

embryo foetus or very early stage of development of a human or animal

first-rate excellent or top class

genes strands of material in cells that tell the body how to develop

HQ headquarters

ID Identity cards

MI5 government department responsible for national security

mutant a creature created by crossing a human and animal genes

Secret Service Government Intelligence Department

stem cell a cell at an early stage of development which can turn into any kind of cell

stem cell technology the use of stem cells to repair damage to the human body

QUIZ

1 Why did Jane Wells kill Professor Hall?

2 What group did the mutants belong to?

3 What does 'Animals Come First' believe?

4 What conference was being held in London?

5 What are the names of the three mutants?

6 Who did Linda Lewis kill?

7 Why is X angry with Commander Watson?

8 What does X do when he is angry?

9 Who told Commander Watson to eliminate the agents?

10 Why did the mutants try to kill the agents?

ABOUT THE AUTHOR

Paul Blum has taught for over 20 years in London inner-city schools.

I wrote The Extraordinary Files for my pupils so they've been tested by some fierce critics (you!). That's why I know you'll enjoy reading them.

I've made the stories edgy in terms of character and content and I've written them using the kind of fast-paced dialogue you'll recognise from television soaps. I hope you'll find The Extraordinary Files an interesting and easy-to-read collection of stories.

ANSWERS TO QUIZ

1 Because he created her as a mutant and she was angry with him

2 Animals Come First

3 That it is wrong to experiment on animals

4 The Gene Genius Conference

5 Jane Wells, Linda Lewis and David Munro

6 Professor Lee

7 Because he thinks Commander Watson has allowed Turnbull and Parker to know too much about the top-secret mutant research

8 He polishes his glasses

9 X

10 Because X told Commander Watson to use the mutants to kill Turnbull and Parker